Ghost Town Treasure

by CLYDE ROBERT BULLA

Illustrated by Robert Shore

SCHOLASTIC INC.
New York Toronto London Auckland Sydney

To
Bengt Nordquist

ISBN 0-590-37955-0

Copyright © 1957 by Clyde Robert Bulla. Illustrations copyright © 1981 by Scholastic Inc. All rights reserved. This edition published by Scholastic Inc., 730 Broadway, New York, N.Y., by arrangement with Thomas Y. Crowell, a division of Harper & Row Pubishers, Inc.

12 11 10 9 8 7 6 5 4 3 2 1   8 9/8 0 1 2 3/9

Contents

A Letter

It was nearly night when the boy came home. He rode up to the old barn at the edge of town. He led his little gray horse inside.

A leather bag was tied to the saddle horn. The boy untied it and set it down in a corner. He took the saddle off the horse.

"Eat your supper, King," he said.

The horse already had his head in the manger. He was eating the hay that was there.

The boy picked up the leather bag and went outside.

The mountains were dark. A mist covered the valley. It was pretty, the boy thought. The town was pretty, too.

Late in the evening it looked almost like any other town. Shadows hid the grass that grew in the streets. No one could see that the houses were empty. No one could see that the stores — all except one — were empty, too.

The boy walked down Main Street. He stopped at the only light in town. It was the light in the grocery store.

He went inside. In the kitchen at the back of the store he found his mother and father.

His father was at the table, reading in the lamplight. His mother was cooking supper.

"Where have you been, Ty?" she asked.

"Up on the mountain," said the boy.

"I wish you wouldn't stay out so late." She saw the leather bag in his hand. "What have you got there?"

"Rocks," he said. "More rocks for my collection. I found some good ones today."

She laughed a little. "Ty Jackson, you're just like a pack rat — always packing things home!"

"The mailman was here," his father told him. "He brought you a letter."

Ty had already seen the letter on the table. He picked it up.

"It's from Paul and Nora!" he said.

He was always glad to have a letter from Paul and Nora. They were almost his best friends, even though they lived a long way off and he had never seen them.

It was strange how they had come to be friends. One day last summer the mailman had brought a letter to the store. On it was written: "To Anyone in Gold Rock, California."

The mailman had given the letter to Ty. It was from a boy and girl in Ohio. They had written:

> We are a brother and sister, 11 and 9 years old. Will someone in Gold Rock write to us? We want to know more about the town because our great-grandfather built the first house there, more than a hundred years ago. He went out west to hunt gold, and he died there. We have the diary he kept. Someday we are coming to California on a visit, and we would like to know someone in Gold Rock.
>
> Yours truly,
> PAUL and NORA CONNOR

Ty had answered the letter. They had written to him. Since then he had sent them more than a dozen letters. They had answered every one.

He sat down at the table and opened their latest letter. He read a little way and sat up straight.

"They're coming out!" he said.

"Who?" asked his mother.

"Paul and Nora. Their father has a vacation. They are all coming out, and Paul and Nora are going to visit me."

He read the letter twice. He began to make plans. "They may be here in about two weeks. Maybe they like to ride horseback. If they do, I'll let them ride King. We can go fishing, too. I can show them my rock collection. They might like to help me hunt rocks. Do you think they would?"

His mother and father said nothing.

"Didn't you hear me?" he asked. "My friends in Ohio are coming."

"We heard you, Ty," said his mother.

"You'll have to write to them as soon as you can," said his father. "You'll have to tell them not to come."

"What do you mean? I *want* them to come," said Ty. "I've *asked* them to."

"I'm sorry about that," said his father.

"But Paul and Nora are my friends. I can't write to them now and tell them not to come. I just can't!"

"You'll have to," said his father, "because in two weeks we won't be living here."

The Ghost Town

It must be a joke, Ty thought. They had always lived in Gold Rock. They had never thought of living anywhere else. He waited for his father to start laughing. But his father did not laugh.

He looked at his mother. She was busy at the stove. She did not turn around.

His father said, "I just had a letter, too. It's from your Uncle Rod. He wants us to come to live with him, and maybe I can get work in a grocery store."

"In the *city?*" asked Ty.

"Yes," said his father.

"But you're not going?" said Ty.

"We have to make a living," said his father, "and a grocery store in a ghost town doesn't help much."

"Gold Rock won't always be a ghost town," said Ty. "People will come back."

"I used to think they would, but I don't anymore," said his father. "When the new highway came through and missed Gold Rock, that was the end of our town. People don't want to live here when they can live in the new town up on the highway."

"This is where I want to live," said Ty. "This is the best place in the world."

His mother came to the table. "Don't you see?" she said. "We can't make a living when there is nobody left to come to the store."

"The people on the ranches come here," said Ty.

"Not anymore," said his mother. "They

go to the stores in the new town."

"What about Mr. Weber?" said Ty. "He has the biggest ranch around here, and he needs lots of groceries."

"Stop and think. How long has it been since he came here?" said his mother. "No, Ty, Mr. Weber is getting his groceries somewhere else. We can't count on him any more."

Ty's father spoke up. "Things won't be so bad. You may like it at Uncle Rod's."

"I *won't* like it," said Ty.

"That's no way to talk," said his mother. "Your uncle is a good man, and he's been good to us. Remember the things he's given you? The boots and the hat and the magnifying glass—"

"I know he's a good man. I never said he wasn't," said Ty, "but I don't want to live in the city. I wouldn't like it, and neither would my horse."

"Oh, Ty, we couldn't take King with us," said his mother. "There wouldn't be any place for him."

"Then I won't go," said Ty.

"Listen to me," said his mother. "We can't always have everything we want. You are old enough to know that. Your father and I don't want to leave Gold Rock any more than you do. This is our home, and we hoped we never would have to leave it. But we've talked it over, and we don't see anything else to do."

"Go if you want to. I'll stay by myself!" Ty pushed back his chair and started out of the kitchen.

His mother called to him. He did not answer. He went out through the store and into the night.

Near the end of Main Street was the old hotel. He sat down on the steps and tried to think.

If they went to live with Uncle Rod, King would have to be sold. Not only that, there would be no one left in Gold Rock. The little town would die.

He looked across the valley to the mountains beyond. An idea came to him. He thought about it for a while. He got up and walked to the edge of town.

Outside the old barn he stopped. "King!" he called softly, so the horse would hear his voice and not be afraid.

He went inside and felt along the wall until he found the saddle.

"King," he said. "Here, boy."

A Night Ride

Ty rode halfway around the mountain. He came to a lane between two rows of pine trees. He rode along under the trees. At the end of the lane were the lights of a ranch house.

He tied King to a post in the yard.

Dogs began to bark. The door opened, and a man looked out.

Ty called to him, "Hello, Mr. Weber. It's Ty Jackson."

"Hello," the man called back. "What brings you out so late?"

"I wanted to see you," said Ty.

"Come in," said Mr. Weber.

He took Ty into his den. It was a big room with Indian rugs and leather chairs.

"Is something wrong?" asked Mr. Weber.

"Yes, sir," said Ty.

"What is it?"

"It's our grocery store," said Ty. "People don't come there any more. They all go to the new town on the highway."

"Why doesn't your father open a store in the new town?" asked Mr. Weber.

"It's too late. The new town already has three grocery stores," said Ty. "Besides, we like Gold Rock. It's our home, and we want to stay. But we'll have to go to the city unless—"

"Unless what?" asked Mr. Weber.

"Unless people start coming to our grocery store again," said Ty. "As long as the people from the ranches came to the store, everything was all right. But now they go to the new town."

"And you want me to buy my groceries at your store?" asked Mr. Weber.

"It would help us if you would," said Ty.

Mr. Weber was quiet for a while. Then he said, "No one takes much care of the Gold Rock road any more. It was slick and muddy the last time I started to your store. I couldn't get my car through. It was easier to go to the new town."

"The road isn't muddy now," said Ty.

"No, but it's rough and rocky," said Mr. Weber. "And there is something else. Your store is a small one. You don't always have the things I need. In the new town I can get everything. You see how it is, don't you?"

Ty nodded. "I'd better go now."

At the door he said, "Maybe I could work for you. If I could work here, I could still live at Gold Rock."

Mr. Weber asked, "How old are you?"

"Twelve," said Ty.

"Twelve is too young for a ranch hand," said Mr. Weber. "I'm sorry. I know how you feel, but it may be a good thing for you to go to the city. A ghost town is no place for a boy."

Ty did not answer. He only said, "Good night."

He rode home. He turned King out to pasture and walked up the dark street to the grocery store. Now he wished he had not gone to Mr. Weber's. It had been a long ride for nothing.

He climbed the stairs to his room over the store. Someone had lit his lamp and turned it low. On his desk were some cookies and a glass of milk.

He looked about him. He was proud of his big oak desk with the top that rolled up and down. He was proud of his rock collection, too. He kept it on two long shelves on the wall above his bunk. Some of the rocks looked like pink glass. Some looked as if they had green moss inside them. Others were blue and yellow and purple. It had taken him a long time to find them.

He was not sure he could take his collection to the city. He knew he could not take his desk. It was too big and heavy.

His mother came up the stairs.

She did not scold him. She did not even ask where he had been. She said, "Are you all right, Ty?"

He nodded.

"Did you find the cookies and milk?" she asked.

He nodded again. When he looked at her, he saw that she had been crying.

He said, "I'll go to the city. It's the best thing to do."

"Your father and I had a talk," she said. "It wouldn't be right for you to go away without seeing your friends."

"Do you mean we can stay?" he asked.

"We can stay till you've had your visit with Paul and Nora." She said good night and went downstairs.

He sat there on the bunk. Paul and Nora were coming, and he could see them, after all. He began to feel better.

He remembered that he had had no supper. He went to the desk and picked up a cookie and the glass of milk.

The Connors

Paul and Nora were on their way. Ty had a card from them. "We will see you soon," it said.

The Jacksons lived in three rooms. There were two rooms back of the store and one above.

Ty's mother said, "There will be Paul and Nora and Mr. and Mrs. Connor. I don't see how they can all stay with us."

"Maybe they could stay at the hotel," said Ty.

It was two years since anyone had lived in the big white Starbuck Hotel, but the furniture was still in the rooms. Mr. Starbuck had left it there when he went away.

"I'll come back someday," he had said to Ty. "Will you look at my place now and then to make sure it's all right? If you will, I'll give you a present."

The present was the big oak desk in Ty's room.

Ty asked his mother, "Could I take my friends to the hotel?"

"Not without asking Mr. Starbuck," said his mother.

"I can't ask him, because I don't know where he is," said Ty. "Maybe they could stay in one of the empty houses."

"That might be better," said his mother.

Ty looked at all the houses in town. Some were old and ready to fall down. Spiders had spun webs in the doorways. Birds had made nests in the chimneys.

But some of the houses were not so old. The windows had not been broken, and the roofs kept out the rain.

Ty chose the house he thought was best. It was a little house that had once been green, but most of the paint was gone. There was a cottonwood tree in the yard and a rosebush by the door.

He swept the walls and scrubbed the floor. He opened the doors and windows to let in the sun and fresh air.

"What shall we do for furniture?" he asked his mother.

"They can have some of ours," she said, "as

soon as we find out what they need."

It took Ty a day to get the house ready.

The next day he went out to the old graveyard a mile from town. Paul and Nora had written that they wanted to see their great-grandfather's grave. Ty had found it under grass and vines. He could read what had been cut into the stone a hundred years ago:

He worked all day cutting weeds and grass.

That night he told his mother and father, "Now I'm ready for my company."

And the next day the Connors were there.

Early in the morning Ty saw the smoke of their campfire. It was on the other side of the creek, near the bridge.

He went toward it. He saw something yellow under the trees across the creek. It was a jeep. Beside it was a tent.

A girl and boy were outside the tent. The girl had a towel in her hand. The boy had a cake of soap. They knelt beside the creek.

The girl said, "We can't wash our hands and

faces here!"

"Yes, we can," said the boy. "Go ahead."

"You go first," she said.

The boy splashed some water on his face. "Ah-h!" He shook his head. "It's cold!"

"I knew it would be," said the girl.

Ty started over the bridge. His shadow fell across the water.

The girl cried out, "There's somebody watching us!"

They saw Ty on the bridge.

The boy jumped to his feet. "It's Ty—I know it is!"

"Yes, it is," said Ty, "and you're Paul and Nora!"

They ran to meet him. They all began to talk at once.

"When did you get here?" asked Ty.

"Last night," said Nora.

"Why didn't you come on into town?"

"It was so late," said Paul, "we didn't want to get you out of bed. We found a good place to camp there under the trees, so we stayed here all night."

"I want to see Gold Rock," said Nora. "I can hardly wait."

"Come on," said Ty. "I'll show you everything."

"You come with us first," said Paul. "I want you to see Mother and Dad."

Ty went with them. A man and woman were busy at the campfire. They smiled and waved when they saw him.

"Good morning, Ty," they said, and they

shook hands with him.

"We like your valley," said Mr. Connor.

"It's beautiful here," said Mrs. Connor.

"Ty is going to have breakfast with us," said Nora.

"No, thank you," said Ty. "I've had breakfast."

"Have another one," said Nora.

"I get so hungry here in the mountains," said Paul, "that I could eat three or four breakfasts. Come on, Ty."

Bacon and eggs were frying. Mrs. Connor had a pot of coffee over the fire. Ty sat down between Paul and Nora. Almost before he knew it, he was eating another breakfast.

A Strange Story

After breakfast, Ty had a ride in the jeep. He rode over the bridge and into town with the Connors. Mr. and Mrs. Connor wanted to stop at the grocery story.

Paul and Nora went with Ty to see the town.

They walked through Gold Rock together. The streets were so quiet that Paul and Nora grew quiet, too.

They stepped over wide cracks in the sidewalks. A toad jumped out of one of the cracks. In a store window a little face looked out at them and was quickly gone.

"What was that?" asked Nora.

"A pack rat," said Ty. "You'll see lots of them here."

They walked past the barber shop and the hotel. They saw the posts where people had once tied their horses. They looked through the window of the old stone jail.

"A place like this makes you think, doesn't

it?" said Paul. "You think how many people used to be here. You wonder why it turned into a ghost town."

"I can tell you why," said Ty. "This used to be a gold town, but people didn't find much gold, and some of them left. Then it was a lumber town. But after a while there weren't enough trees to keep the lumber mill running, so more people went away. Then the new highway came through and missed us, and that was the end of Gold Rock."

"Why was it the end?" asked Nora.

"My father says there is nothing to keep people here anymore," said Ty. "They don't want to live here when they can live in the new town on the highway."

"I'd rather live in Gold Rock," said Paul.

"So would I," said Nora. "It's so pretty here. It looks just the way Grandfather Connor wrote about it in his diary."

"We brought this diary with us," said Paul. "We thought you'd like to see it."

While they walked through town, he and

Nora told Ty about their great-grandfather.

"He left his wife and children in Ohio and came here to find gold," said Nora. "He was going to send for them when he struck it rich."

"But he never struck it rich," said Paul. "Sometimes he was up in the mountains or the canyon for days at a time, looking for gold. He did find something, but it wasn't gold."

"What did he find?" asked Ty.

"A cave," said Paul, "a cave in the canyon."

Nora asked Ty, "Do you know where it is?"

He shook his head. "I've never heard of any cave in the canyon."

"Maybe no one else ever found it," said Paul. "Here is all we know about it. Grandfather made his last trip into the canyon, and he was gone so long that his friends went out to look for him. They found him just outside the canyon. He was trying to get back to

town, but he was too weak to walk. He said something about a cave and being lost a long time with nothing to eat. That was all he said before he died. His friends wrote his family about it and sent his diary."

It was a strange story. Ty kept thinking about it while he showed them the little house where they were to stay. He was still thinking about it when he took them to the pasture to see King.

"He's a beautiful horse," said Nora.

"He's gentle, too," said Paul.

And the next minute, King reached out and bit Paul on the shoulder!

"King!" shouted Ty.

King ran a little way off. He rolled his eyes and pawed the dirt.

Ty said to Paul, "He didn't hurt you, did he?"

Paul felt his shoulder. "No. It didn't hurt at all. It just surprised me."

"That's a trick he has," said Ty. "He likes to play. Sometimes he pretends to bite me, but he just bites with his lips. Look at him, playing he's a wild horse."

Paul and Nora were laughing.

"He's funny," said Nora.

"Some people might not think so," said Ty. "They might even whip him when he plays his tricks, and no one has ever whipped him. I'm afraid when I sell him —" He stopped.

Paul said, "You wouldn't ever sell him, would you?"

"I have to sell him," said Ty. "I can't keep him much longer."

He told them why.

Nora asked, "Isn't there *any* way you can keep your horse?"

"No," said Ty.

"It's too bad," said Paul. "I know how I'd feel if I had to give up my horse and my home, too."

"There's no use talking about it," said Ty. "Let's forget all about it while you're here and have all the fun we can."

But he could not forget about it, and neither could Paul and Nora.

Diary of John Connor

The next day the Connors moved to the house Ty had made ready for them. There was not much moving to do. They only took down the tent and drove the jeep up into the yard.

Ty had brought some chairs and a small table from home.

"I wish I had some beds for you," he said.

"We don't need beds," said Paul. "We camped out all the way to California. We slept on the ground, and it was fun."

"But I'm glad we have this house," said

Nora. "Mother says she likes a roof over her head at night."

"I'm glad we have a roof over our heads," said Paul, "because it looks like rain today."

They looked at the clouds over the mountains.

"I don't think it's going to rain for an hour or two," said Ty. "We'll have time to go out to the graveyard."

Nora picked some yellow roses from the bush by the house. She and Paul and Ty walked out to the old graveyard.

Paul found the stone. "See, Nora? It says 'John Connor.'"

She laid the flowers on the grave.

"This is a lonesome place," said Paul.

"It's pretty, with all the trees," said Nora, "but it *is* lonesome."

"Let's go back," said Paul.

"We'd *better* go back," said Ty. "Those clouds are coming up fast."

They started toward town. The sky grew darker.

They began to run. They ran into the

grocery store just as the first big drops of rain were falling.

"I didn't want it to rain!" said Nora. "Now the day is spoiled."

"No, it isn't," said Paul. "This is a good time to see Ty's rock collection."

Ty took them up to his room. He showed them his shelves of rocks.

"Do you know the names of all these?" asked Paul.

"I know most of them," said Ty. "Some friends of mine, Fritz and Stevie, told me the names. They used to live here, and they know all about rocks."

He took his magnifying glass out of the desk. "My uncle sent me this so I could look at my collection through it," he said. "Try it. It brings out more colors."

Paul and Nora took turns looking at the rocks through the magnifying glass.

"I'd like to start a collection," said Paul, "if I could find rocks like these."

"You can find them," said Ty. "I'll help you."

By the time they had looked at all the rocks, the rain had almost stopped.

"This would be a good day to look at Grandfather Connor's diary," said Paul. "Would you like to see it?"

"Yes, I would," said Ty.

Paul ran out and brought back the diary. It was a little brown book. On the front was printed, "Diary of John Connor."

"He took this with him wherever he went," said Paul. "He wrote in it every day."

The book was so old it was falling apart. Ty was very careful with it. He read the first page:

March 19, 1858

Today the others are at the creek, panning for gold. I think there is little gold in the creek, but I believe there is much to be found near here. There are now ten houses in the town of Gold Rock. Mine was the first one built. How I miss my dear wife and children! How happy I will be when we are together in this beautiful valley!

"Where is the part about the cave?" asked Ty.

"At the very end. I'll show you," said Paul. "This book must have been left open in the rain, because the writing is faded at the end. We can't read it all, but here it says: 'The cave is in the canyon not far from town. Many people must have gone near it, yet it is well hidden. I found it only because I went after my shovel, which had fallen down the bank. I was afraid I could not find this wonderful cave again, so I put marks on the trees nearby. I saw, too, that it is just beneath the Great Cross. I shall camp in the canyon tonight and go back to the cave in the morning.' And that is the end."

"Here is a little more on the last page," said Ty.

"We can't read that part," said Paul. "It's faded out, all but a word or two."

Ty looked at the end of the diary. He could make out a few of the faded letters. "Did anyone ever try to read this through a magnifying glass?" he asked.

"I don't know," said Nora.

"I don't think so," said Paul.

Ty held the glass over the last page. "It's something about the cave."

He went to the window where the light was better. He began to spell the words to himself. He stopped.

He stood there so long that Paul asked, "What's the matter?"

Ty handed him the diary and the glass. "Look!" he said.

"Could you read it?" asked Paul.

"Yes," said Ty.

"What does it say?" asked Nora. "Tell us!"

He told them. He was so excited he could hardly speak the words. "It says 'gold in the cave.'"

Ideas

Paul held the magnifying glass over the diary. Nora tried to look over his shoulder.

He said, "I think you're right, Ty. That's what it looks like."

" 'Gold in the cave,' " said Nora.

"We'd better keep this a secret," said Ty.

"I won't tell," she said.

"Let's tell our fathers and mothers," said Paul.

"All right," said Ty.

"Grandfather *did* find gold," said Nora, "and then he died before he could tell anyone."

She went to the window. The rain had stopped. "Can we go now?" she asked.

"Where?" asked Paul.

"To the cave."

"We don't know where it is," said Paul.

"Yes, we do. It's in the canyon."

"It's a big canyon," said Paul.

"The diary tells where to find it." She was reading in the little book. "Here it says the cave is in the canyon just beneath the Great Cross." She asked Ty, "Where is the Great Cross?"

"I don't know," he said. "I never heard of it before."

"Maybe your father would know," said Paul.

They ran downstairs.

Ty's father was in the store.

"Mr. Jackson, this old book is Grandfather Connor's diary," said Nora, "and we just found something in it — "

"Read this part at the end," said Ty.

"Read it to me," said his father. "Your eyes are better than mine."

"It tells how he found a cave in the canyon," said Ty. "At the very end it says 'gold in the cave.' "

"It says the cave is just beneath the Great Cross," said Paul. "What does that mean, Mr. Jackson?"

"The Great Cross?" said Ty's father. "I

don't know."

"Whatever it is, we'll find it," said Ty.

His father told him, "Don't forget, all this happened over a hundred years ago. Lots of people have looked for gold in the canyon. If there was a cave with gold in it, wouldn't someone else have found it before now?"

"Maybe," said Ty, "and maybe not."

"It's all right if we look, isn't it?" asked Paul.

"Of course it is," said Mr. Jackson. "Just remember that lots of people start out looking for gold, but not many ever find it. If you don't find the cave with gold in it, I don't want you to be too disappointed."

Paul and Nora went to tell their mother and father what they had found in the diary. When they came back to the store, Nora told Ty, "They weren't excited at all."

Paul said, "They thought the same as your father. They thought because it all happened over a hundred years ago, no one could find the cave now."

"The diary says it's not far from town, just

under the Great Cross," said Nora. "All we have to do is find the Great Cross."

"But we don't know where the Great Cross is," said Paul. "We don't even know *what* it is."

"We can't find the cave if we don't go look for it," said Nora.

"We'd better not start today," said Ty. "It's a little too late, and it isn't good to be caught in the canyon after dark. Let's start out early in the morning."

"All right," said Nora. "Then we'll have all day."

Ty told her and Paul, "Keep thinking about the Great Cross. Try to get some ideas."

Ty kept thinking, too. That night, after he had gone to bed, an idea came to him. He lay there and thought about it. Then, just as he was going to sleep, another idea came.

For a long time he lay there, thinking hard.

The Gold Hunters

Early the next morning Ty and Paul and Nora were ready to go.

Ty told his mother, "We may be gone all day."

"Then you'd better bring lunch," she said.

She gave them each a sandwich and an apple.

"There go the gold hunters," said Mrs. Connor, as they started down the street, and she called, "Good-bye."

"Good luck," called Mr. Connor.

"They don't really think we're going to find gold," said Paul.

"We may surprise them," said Nora.

"Last night I had an idea about the Great Cross," said Ty. "There are animal trails in the canyon, and there are places where they cross one another. One of those places might be the Great Cross."

"Grandfather found the cave over a hundred years ago," said Paul. "Maybe the trails have changed by now."

"My father says animal trails don't change much. In a wild place like the canyon, animals follow the same trails for years and years. And I thought of something else," said Ty. "If we find the cave with gold in it, it will cause a gold rush."

"Like the California gold rush in 1849?" asked Paul.

"Yes," said Ty. "It always happens when anyone finds gold. People rush to the place and try to find more. So many people will come to Gold Rock, and it won't be a ghost town anymore. Do you see what that will mean?"

"What will it mean?" asked Nora.

"I see!" said Paul. "If it's not a ghost town, you won't have to go away."

"That's right. I won't have to go away," said Ty.

"Oh, I hope we find the gold," said Nora. "I hope we find it today!"

They walked along the creek bank. The creek led into the canyon.

The sun was bright on the canyon walls. Trees and bushes and rocks covered the canyon floor. A trail ran up through the trees.

They followed the trail. Pine needles were thick under their feet. Among the needles they could see the tracks of deer and rabbits.

"Here's another trail," said Ty.

They stopped where the two trails crossed.

"This must be the place," said Nora.

They looked all about them.

"Do you remember what Grandfather Connor wrote in his diary?" asked Paul. "He dropped his shovel down a bank and went after it. That's how he found the cave. But there's no bank here."

"No, there isn't," said Ty. "Let's go on to the next cross."

The trail grew steep. Their feet slipped on the pine needles. It was hard for Nora to keep up.

Paul took her by the hand and pulled her

along. At the next cross-trail she sat down to rest.

"This looks more like the place," said Ty.

"Here's a bank," said Paul. "It *could* be where Grandfather dropped his shovel."

The boys climbed down the bank. They held to roots and vines to keep from sliding all the way to the bottom.

Ty looked on one side. Paul looked on the other.

"If there is a cave here, I can't see it," said Paul.

"The diary says it is well hidden," said Ty.

For a long time they looked. They grew hot and tired. Paul tore his shirt, and a red ant stung Ty on the hand.

They gave up at last. They climbed back to the trail.

They were quiet as they ate lunch.

There was a spring not far away. They lay down and drank the clear, cold water as it ran down over the rocks.

Paul asked Ty, "What shall we do?"

Ty did not answer.

"I thought it would be easy to find the cave," said Nora.

"Shall we go on to the next place where the trails cross?" asked Paul.

Ty said, "Maybe I had the wrong idea. Maybe the Great Cross isn't a cross in the trails at all."

"What else could it be?" asked Nora.

"I don't know," said Ty.

"It would take years to look everywhere in this canyon," said Paul.

They started home. They were tired and

disappointed. Ty was the most disappointed of all.

Paul tried to make him feel better. "I'm glad we came to the canyon," he said. "I never saw so many rocks before. When I start my collection, I'm coming back here."

Nora found a purple stone in the side of a big rock. "This is pretty," she said, "but you couldn't ever get it out."

"Yes, you could," said Ty. "I can get it for you. I can take a hammer and chisel and cut it out."

"I'd like to have it," said Paul. "Can we come back tomorrow?"

"Maybe," said Ty. He led the way out of the canyon.

"Now I know how the gold hunters used to feel," said Nora, "when they looked for gold and didn't find any."

"Let's not talk about it, Nora," said Paul.

"No," said Ty. "Let's just forget all about it."

Shadows on the Rocks

Days went by. No one spoke of the cave in the canyon.

Ty taught Paul and Nora to fish, and they fished in the creek. They took turns riding King. They went mountain climbing.

Nora said one afternoon, "I wish we could stay all summer."

"So do I," said Paul, "but pretty soon we'll be on our way home. And I haven't started my rock collection yet."

"We'll start it now," said Ty.

They walked along the creek and picked up rocks as they went. Now and then Ty used his hammer and chisel to cut a stone out of a larger rock.

"Do you remember the purple stone I saw in the canyon?" asked Nora.

"Yes," said Paul. "Can we get it now?"

"We can if we hurry," said Ty. "But if we

get caught in the canyon after dark, we might not find our way out until morning."

They followed the creek into the canyon.

They walked up the trail. In the late afternoon the canyon was filled with shadows. The high canyon walls kept out the sun.

Paul found the big gray rock with the small purple stone in its side. Ty set to work with his hammer and chisel. He cut out the small stone and gave it to Paul.

They started down the trail.

Nora was behind. One of her shoelaces came untied.

"Wait," she said, but no one heard her.

She stepped on the shoelace. Her shoe flew off, and she fell down.

"Wait!" she cried.

This time Ty and Paul heard her. They came back.

"Are you all right?" asked Paul.

"I think so," she said.

Ty found her shoe and gave it to her.

Nora did not get up. She sat there in the trail. She was looking back into the canyon.

"Come on. Hurry," said Paul.

"Look!" she said, and she pointed.

They looked.

Down the side of the canyon wall was a long ridge. A shelf of rock cut across it. In the shadows of evening the two lines made a cross.

"The Great Cross!" said Nora.

Ty and Paul stood still, looking at the canyon wall.

"I've lived here all my life and I've seen that cliff a hundred times," said Ty, "but I

never saw the cross before."

"You have to be in the right place at the right time," said Paul.

"And the right time is evening," said Ty, "when the shadows are on the rocks."

"It's changing now," said Nora. "Maybe we won't be able to find it again when all the shadows have changed."

"You wait here," said Ty. He ran up the trail.

"Where is he going?" asked Nora.

Paul shook his head.

She put on her shoe and got up. They watched the shadows move across the cliff.

"It doesn't look so much like a cross now," she said.

"Ty says it gets dark fast up here," said Paul.

A cool wind blew through the canyon. Pine needles fell with a sound like rain.

"I wish he hadn't gone," said Nora.

"I wish he would hurry," said Paul. "We don't want to stay here all night."

They heard running steps.

Ty came in sight. "Let's go," he said.

They ran down the trail. They came to the creek and followed it out of the canyon.

In the valley there was more daylight left. They could see Gold Rock ahead.

Paul asked Ty, "Where were you, back in the canyon?"

"I went up the trail till I was right under the cross," said Ty. "I put a mark on a tree with my chisel. I wanted to be sure we could find the place in the morning!"

Back to the Canyon

The sun was just over the mountain when they started out the next morning.

"My father told us to bring him a pocketful of gold," said Paul, "but he was joking."

"Nobody thinks we are going to find it," said Nora. "Nobody but us."

"We *are* going to find it," said Ty. "We're on the right track."

They came to the mouth of the canyon. In the morning light they could not see the Great Cross on the canyon wall.

"But we know where it is," said Ty.

They climbed the trail, past the big rock where Ty had cut out the purple stone. They climbed until they were close to the canyon wall. At the edge of the trail was a cedar tree. On the trunk was the mark Ty had made with his chisel.

"This tree is just below the Great Cross," he said.

"Grandfather was here when he dropped his shovel," said Paul.

"And this is the bank he climbed down to find it," said Nora.

The bank was not very steep, but it was rocky and covered with bushes.

Paul told Nora, "You'd better wait up here."

"It isn't too steep for me," she said. "I want to help look."

They climbed down together. They looked among bushes and rocks.

Paul said at last, "We've been down the bank from top to bottom. Where is the cave?"

"Sometimes there are rock slides in the canyon," said Ty. "Maybe rocks have slid down and covered the cave."

"Then how can we ever find it?" asked Paul.

Ty broke three sticks off a small, dead bush. "Let's take these and dig in the side of the bank. If we dig in enough places, maybe we can find the cave."

They climbed up the bank, digging as they went.

"All I can find is rocks and dirt," said Paul.

Nora sat down to rest. She leaned against a rock. "That's funny," she said. She put her hand behind her.

"What's funny?" asked Paul.

"I felt something cool on the back of my neck."

Ty asked quickly, "Where?"

"Right here," said Nora. "It's cool air. I

can feel it between these two big rocks."

Ty looked at the rocks. He tried to pull them apart, but they were too big and heavy.

At the foot of the bank he found a strong pine branch. It looked as if it had been torn from a tree by a storm. He dragged it up the bank. He pushed the end of it between the two rocks.

With the branch, he began to pry the rocks apart. Paul helped him. Slowly the rocks moved. One came free and rolled down the bank.

They jumped aside to get out of the way.
Nora cried out. There in the side of the bank
was a dark, deep hole.

"We've found it!" said Paul.

They looked into the cave.

"Maybe it's an old gold mine," said Nora.

"It's so dark," said Paul, "I can see only a
little way."

"We have candles in the store," said Ty. "You and Nora stay here, and I'll go get them."

Before they could answer, he was on his way. He ran all the way back to Gold Rock.

By Candlelight

Ty's father was in the store. He listened to what Ty had to tell him.

While they were talking, Mr. Connor came into the store. "Where are Nora and Paul?" he asked.

"In the canyon," said Ty, "at the cave."

Mr. Connor stared at him. "The *cave*?"

"Yes. We found it," said Ty. "It goes right into the side of the bank."

"I'm going up with him now." Ty's father had a box of candles in one hand and a long rope in the other.

"I'm going, too," said Mr. Connor.

They set out for the canyon. The two men were as excited as Ty. Mr. Connor kept saying, "So you really found it!"

They climbed the canyon trail.

"The Great Cross is there on the cliff," said Ty.

"I don't see it," said Mr. Connor.

"You can't see it now, but it's there."

They came to the cedar tree Ty had marked. They climbed down the bank to where Paul and Nora were waiting.

The two men looked into the cave.

Ty's father asked Paul and Nora, "Did you go inside it?"

They shook their heads.

"I was afraid," said Nora.

"And it was too dark for us to see anything," said Paul.

"I'm glad you waited," said Ty's father, "because the cave might not be safe. There might be falling rocks or pools of water."

He tied one end of the rope under his arms. He took a candle out of the box and lighted it.

"I'll leave the other end of the rope here," he said. "If I get into trouble, you can pull me out."

He went into the cave. He was gone only

a few minutes, but it seemed a long time to Ty and Paul and Nora.

When he came out, there was a strange look on his face.

"It's safe enough," he said. "Come on, all of you. I want you to see this."

Each took a lighted candle. The two men went ahead. Paul and Nora and Ty went after them.

At first the way was narrow. Then it grew wider until it opened into a large room.

The candlelight shone on something that looked like a great waterfall. It sparkled with color — silver and red-brown and blue. But it was not water. It was all of stone.

"It's a natural cave!" said Mr. Connor.

Nora looked over her head.

"Stone icicles," she said.

Paul pointed to the floor. "And more stone icicles going up to meet them," he said.

"This is only part of the cave," said Ty's father. "There are rooms beyond this."

"Grandfather must have been lost here," said Mr. Connor. "It must have taken him

days to find his way out."

"He could have had water," said Paul. "See how it drips off the rocks?"

"Water, yes," said Mr. Connor, "but no food."

Nora pulled her collar up around her neck. "I'm cold," she said.

"So am I," said Paul

"It's too cold to stay here long without warmer clothes," said Ty's father.

They climbed out of the cave.

"We forgot something," said Ty. "We forgot to look for the gold."

"It was such a wonderful sight," said Mr. Connor, "that I didn't think about gold."

"Neither did I," said Ty's father.

"But there *must* be gold," said Paul. "Grandfather said there was."

Ty's father sat in the sun until he was warm again. Then he went back into the cave. He came out with his pockets full of rocks.

"We'll look at these," he said, "and see how much gold we can find."

Fritz and Stevie

Back in town, Ty's father took a hammer and broke the rock samples into small pieces. He spread them out on the back step.

"There may be gold here," he said, "but I don't see any."

"I don't know much about gold," said Mr. Connor.

Ty's father said, "We'd better find someone who knows more about it than we do."

"Do you know someone?" asked Mr. Connor.

"Yes, I do," said Ty's father.

"Fritz and Stevie?" asked Ty.

"Yes," said his father.

"Fritz and Stevie are friends of ours," Ty told Paul and Nora, "and we can trust them. They lived here for a while, but now they live in the new town. They went to school and learned about rocks and gold and things like that."

The men drove off in the jeep. Before long they were back. Fritz and Stevie were behind them on a motorcycle.

Fritz and Stevie were brothers. They were young men, tall and strong, with brown faces.

"We want to see the cave," said Fritz.

"We'll let you know what we find," said Stevie.

They spent four days in the cave. When they came back to Gold Rock, they stopped at the grocery store. The Connors and Jacksons were waiting to see what they had found.

"We've been all over the cave," Stevie told them.

"What did you find?" asked Ty.

"We found lots of rocks and lots of rooms," said Fritz.

"And gold?" asked Ty.

"No," said Fritz.

"We didn't find a sign of it," said Stevie.

"But there *is* gold," said Paul.

"What makes you so sure of that?" asked Stevie.

"Our grandfather kept a diary," said Paul. "He found the cave, and he wrote about the gold."

"I'd like to see what he wrote," said Fritz.

Paul brought the diary to the store.

Fritz and Stevie looked through it.

"Here is the part about finding the cave," said Fritz, "but I don't see anything about gold."

Paul showed him the last page. "See here, where the writing is all faded? We couldn't read it until Ty looked at it with his magnifying glass. It says 'gold in the cave.'"

Stevie took a leather case out of his pocket. In it was a small magnifying glass made to fit over one eye. It was the glass he used to study rock samples.

"This is a good, strong one," he said.

He put the glass to his eye and bent over the diary. He took a long look, then he handed the book and the glass to his brother.

Fritz looked at the last page of the diary. He said, "I see."

"It's a little scratch on the paper," said Stevie. "It makes the *c* look like a *g*. Look, Paul."

Paul took the diary and put the glass to his eye. "Oh," he said.

"What is it?" asked Nora.

"It's not 'gold in the cave,' " said Paul. "It says '*cold* in the cave.' "

"That's what it says," said Stevie. " 'Cold in the cave.' I'm sorry."

While the others were talking, Ty turned and went outside. He didn't want to talk. He didn't want to see anyone.

He stood at the end of Main Street. He looked at the mountains, the valley, the houses at the edge of Gold Rock.

He went on out to the old barn. His horse was eating grass outside.

"There isn't any gold, King," he said. "There isn't any at all, and we have to go away."

He put his head against the horse's side.

Paul and Nora had followed him. In sight of the barn, they stopped.

"Maybe — maybe he doesn't want to talk to anyone now," she said.

"No, I don't think he does," said Paul.

They turned and went slowly back to the grocery store.

In the Grocery Store

The next day was the Connors' last day in Gold Rock. Their suitcases were packed and in the jeep.

Nora said to Ty, "We've had a wonderful time."

"Our father says we can come back next year." Paul looked at Ty. "But you won't be here, will you?"

"No," said Ty. "We'll be gone in another week."

"Anyway, you'll write to us, won't you?" asked Nora.

"Yes, I'll write," said Ty.

The Connors and the Jacksons said good-bye to one another. The jeep drove out of town and over the bridge. Ty watched until it was out of sight.

He went into the store. It was quiet with Paul and Nora gone. He did not know what to do.

As he started up to his room, he heard a car drive into town.

It was the Connors coming back, he thought. They must have forgotten something.

He ran to the door. The car outside was not the Connors' jeep. It was a long black car with "Weber's Ranch" on the side. Mr. Weber was at the wheel.

"Hello, Ty," he said.

"Hello, Mr. Weber." Ty came out of the store.

"I haven't seen you since the night you rode your horse up to the ranch," said Mr. Weber. "How have you been?"

"All right, thank you," said Ty.

"I heard some news," said Mr. Weber. "I

drove over to find out if it's true."

"It's true that we are going to leave Gold Rock," Ty told him. "Is that what you mean?"

Mr. Weber shook his head. "I heard something about a cave in the canyon. Did you really find one?"

"Yes, we did," said Ty.

"Could I see it?" asked Mr. Weber.

"Yes, I'll take you up there," said Ty.

He walked into the canyon with Mr. Weber. He led him into the cave. By candlelight they looked at the great stone waterfall and the stone icicles.

All the way back to town Mr. Weber talked about the cave. "It's a wonderful sight!" he said.

When they got back to Gold Rock, two more cars were waiting. In the cars were people Ty had never seen before.

A woman asked him, "Are you the boy who found the cave?"

"I helped find it," he said.

"Will you take us up there?" she asked.

"We'll pay you to be our guide."

There were nine people in the cars. Ty guided them to the cave.

When they came back to town, another car was waiting. A man called to him, "Where is this cave everyone is talking about?"

Before the day was over, Ty had taken twenty people to see the cave.

The next day more people came to Gold Rock. Two of them were from a newspaper. One of them took pictures of the cave. The other wrote a story about it.

After that, even more people came to Gold Rock. Some of them said, "I read about the cave in the paper."

One day a neat little man with a gray mustache came to the store.

"Do you know me, Ty?" he asked.

"It's Mr. Starbuck!" said Ty. "I still have the desk you gave me."

"Did you take good care of my hotel while I was gone?" asked the man.

"It's just as good as ever," said Ty.

"I've been hearing about the cave in the canyon," said Mr. Starbuck. "I hear a lot of people have been coming to see it."

"Yes, they have," said Ty. "Look at all the cars on Main Street."

"Maybe some of them would like a place to stay," said Mr. Starbuck. "Maybe I'll open my hotel again."

A woman came into the store. She asked Ty, "Will you wait on me? We're going to see the cave, and we want some things for a picnic lunch. I want a loaf of bread and some peanut butter and some of these nice tomatoes."

"Will that be all?" asked Ty.

"Have you any fresh eggs?" asked the woman.

"Not now," said Ty, "but we'll have some in about an hour, when my father gets back with the grocery truck."

The woman paid for the groceries and went out.

Mr. Starbuck asked, "How is the grocery business?"

"Business is good," said Ty. "Father says if it would stay this good, we wouldn't have to leave Gold Rock."

"What do you mean — if it would stay this good?" said Mr. Starbuck. "It's going to get better and better. People are coming from all over the country to see the cave. I hear the canyon is going to be a state park someday."

"Do you think it *will*?" asked Ty.

"I wouldn't be surprised." Mr. Starbuck went down the street toward his hotel.

Ty found some paper under the counter. He took the pencil from behind his ear and began to write:

Dear Paul and Nora,

There isn't time for me to write much, but I want to tell you that Gold Rock is not a ghost town anymore. You never saw a town come to life so fast. People are coming here to see the cave. It looks as if they will keep coming. It looks as if we will be here when you come back next summer —

He stopped writing. The woman had come back into the store.

"I forgot to get a dozen apples," she said.

He put them in a sack for her.

She gave him a sharp look. "Young man, is there something funny about me?"

"Oh, no," he said.

"Then what are you smiling for?" she asked.

"I didn't know I was smiling," he said. "I suppose it's because I feel so good."

She took the apples and went out.

Long after she was gone, Ty stood there smiling as he listened to the voices in the street outside.